CoW

FINDS a Friend

For Josie

Cow Finds a Friend

Copyright © 2003 Todd Aaron Smith

New Kids Media™ is published by Baker Book House Company, P.O. Box 6287, Grand Rapids, MI 49516-6287

ISBN 0-8010-4516-9

Printed in China

1 2 3 4 5 6 7 – 06 05 04 03

Visit Cowontheweb.com

CoW
Finds a Friend

Todd Aaron Smith

BAKER
A DIVISION OF
Baker Book House Co

Cow loved to wander in the field outside the barn. Late one afternoon, on one of her usual strolls, she found herself at the top of the hill. What a good place, she thought, to let out a loud "MOOO."

"MOOO," Cow said, loud and clear. She always listened for the ring of her MOOOs, and the beautiful silence that always followed.

But this day she didn't hear silence. She heard a MOOO echo back! Cow didn't know sounds could bounce back. Was another cow calling to her?

Cow answered. "MOOO!"

Curiosity got the best of Cow. *Who could be back in those trees?* she wondered. Cow inched closer and stepped into the woods.

As she wandered into the woods, she called, "Hello? Hello?" But no one answered. "MOOO," Cow tried again, wandering deeper into the woods.

Now Cow could only hear silence. She saw the sun fade and darkness fall. Suddenly Cow realized she had walked so far, she didn't know how to get back to the farm.

Cow began to hear all sorts of strange sounds, night noises that she didn't recognize. She felt a little scared, but remembered God's care and how he promises to bring us comfort. He will even walk with us everywhere we go. "Thank you, God," Cow started to pray.

A tiny voice interrupted. "Howdy!" said a black-masked critter.

"Well, hello, Mr. Raccoon," Cow said. "Can you help me? I'm afraid I'm lost! I was looking for a cow I heard mooing in the woods, but I can't seem to find her."

"Another cow?" asked Mr. Raccoon. "Hmph. I've never seen another cow in the woods. Now that I think about it, I've never seen you here before, either!"

"I've never been here this late," Cow said.

"Oh, that explains it," Mr. Raccoon answered. "I sleep during the day and only come out at night."

While Mr. Raccoon couldn't tell Cow how to get back to the farm, he did warn Cow to stay completely away from that big, old, fallen tree: "That's where the skunk lives, and he's very stinky and mean! Nobody likes that skunk!"

"Oh," Cow said. "Thanks." Now she really felt scared.

Cow began to hurry to find the way home.
Suddenly she saw a little brown bat hanging upside
down from a tree branch. "Excuse me, please,"
Cow asked, "Do you know where the farm is?"

"Well, whatever you do," Bat said, "stay away from that stinky skunk that lives near that fallen tree! That skunk's not nice at all! God must have made a big mistake when he made skunks!"

A mistake? wondered Cow. *Did God make a mistake?*

"Just remember what I said about that skunk!" called Bat as he spread his wings and flew up and over the trees.

Cow walked on through the dark woods. Suddenly she saw a big creature ahead . . . but it wasn't another cow! Cow shivered. Was it the mean skunk?

No, Cow decided, that creature looks bigger than a skunk . . . in fact, it looks like my friend Sheep's cute, cuddly teddy bear. That was it! A bear! "Well, Cow said to herself," The bigger the bear, the cuddlier it must be. "She called to it, "Hello, Bear!"

"Grrr!" the bear growled. Cow froze. *This bear isn't cute or cuddly,* she thought. The bear growled again and lunged at Cow.

What am I going to do?

Before Cow could think of something, the bear started to chase her! Cow ran, her heart pounding as fast as her legs.

But the bear could run faster than Cow, and he cornered her by some trees. Cow was trapped! The bear moved closer.

Cow braced herself as the bear stood on its hind legs and started to pounce . . .

Just then, from behind a tree, a skunk jumped between Cow and the bear. With lightning speed, the skunk turned and sprayed the bear. Shocked, the bear howled loudly and ran off into the woods!

"Oh no!" Cow cried. "Will the stinky, mean skunk spray me too?" The skunk turned and smiled. "Are you okay?" he asked.

"Y-y-yes," stammered Cow. She couldn't help but feel surprised. "Y-y-you helped me! You're not mean. You're friendly!"

"We better get you home," Skunk said. "I know just where the farm is, and I'll be glad to take you there."

Following Skunk at a distance, Cow said: "Mr. Raccoon and Bat were wrong. You aren't mean, just a little stinky . . . but at the right moment. If you hadn't sprayed that bear, I might be hamburger! I guess God doesn't make mistakes in how we're made!"

"We can make mistakes in how we act, though," Skunk said. "I may be stinky, but that's how God made me, so I want to be good and stinky."

Cow thought about the other important lessons learned this day: To not believe everything you hear, and to not judge others simply by how they look.

On the hill at the edge of the woods, Cow stopped her new friend. "Thank you for being exactly as God made you," she said.

The words echoed from the woods.
"You can say that again," Skunk said.
"Again . . . ," his voice echoed, "again . . . ."

As Cow walked home, she said, "And thank you, God, for being exactly who You are. You give me new friends, but you are the best friend."